The King's Carriage

Written & Illustrated

Lexia G Mackin

ELGEM BOOKS

Toowoomba, QLD. Australia.

www.elgembooks.com

ISBN: 978-0-9757679-5-5

Dedication

Threaded through time, the hand of God reaches down and touches certain individuals and the world is never the same. The prophet, Bill Britton (1918-1985), is one of those men.

This story is based on one of the prophecies he gave, "The Harness of the Lord".

It is a prophecy worthy of being kept alive.

This book is dedicated to

Bill Britton

and the Lord, who gave the prophecy.

Other books:

Children's books:
I Hate Reading!

Adult Books
Help! I'm a Mum

Coming soon:
Help! I'm a Dad

Check them out
www.elgembooks.com

Contents

Write a Review . . . vi

1. An Unusual Birth . . . 1

2. The Blessing . . . 9

3. Wild and Free . . . 17

4. An Important Visitor . . . 23

5. A New Day Dawns . . . 33

6. Training Begins . . . 41

7. Disaster . . . 51

8. Heart's Response . . . 63

9. Now or Never . . . 71

10. The King is Coming . . . 77

11. The Cost of Freedom . . . 83

Write a Review

Authors live by the reviews that are placed on the website. As you add a review, more people get to see the book, and the message of the Kingdom is extended.

The book is available on Amazon and through the Elgem Books website, at www.elgembooks.com.

1. An Unusual Birth

Avram stood tall and proud on the top of the hill looking over his band of mares, his glossy black coat glistening in the sunlight, his tail raised slightly in the soft breeze caressing him. He stood nineteen hands high, from the ground to the top of his withers. He had a strikingly broad head, with forward focussed ears, alert to all the sounds around him. His eyes, which were prominent in his broad forehead, communicated intelligence and spirit.

Mystery surrounds Avram's origins. While it is essential for him to have had a mother and father, a dam and a sire, no-one quite knows who they were. There is no-one to say which mare he was "out of", nor which sire he was "by". Some say he came from a province south-west of France but, as tradition would show, those who did were predominantly grey or white, a factor not lost when observing the sleek black of Avram.

He reigned supreme over a herd of horses, a herd that belonged to the King. Each horse in the herd showed the same spirit as Avram, the same long, arched neck that flowed gracefully into well-defined withers. Most of the herd carried the traditional grey, in varying shades, but always with a silver sheen.

The herd was kept in a pasture full of sweet, green grass and wildflowers. There was a stream of fresh water flowing through the field. It was so cool and refreshing, especially on a hot summer's day. Each horse was able to drink deeply from the softly flowing water, never diminishing the supply that flowed through. It was a place of joy and contentment. New foals were being born; mares were well nourished to feed their foals;

retired horses were able to enjoy their last days in the beauty of nature; and the young colts, eager to race and test their strength, were able to run and frolic in abandonment with never a care in the world.

Occasionally, the King would send a steward to choose a horse for his stables. Blessed was the one that was chosen. Avram, himself, had been chosen for service to the King, many sun-cycles ago. He was retired now but held his days of service in his memory like a shrine. Those not chosen for kingly service were, none the less, selected for other positions of honour within the royal palace, often for some high ranking official in the king's service.

Most people only see a horse as a beast of burden, but there is much more to a horse than its ability to carry. Horses seem to carry a "sixth sense". They often understand the deepest need of a person in trouble; they can exhibit an other-worldly patience and understanding toward a less-formed or socially inadequate person—those of whom the world of men has rejected.

Avram was one who had a strong sixth sense. He was able to see what was under the surface and had a canny knack of seeing a person's pain. He was from a line of horses who, in the horse world, were called the Remnant.

The Remnants knew the times and the seasons; they could hear the Voice when He spoke; they could predict; they could understand; they had wisdom beyond their natural ability. There was a time, long, long ago, when all horses had this ability, but most of them had lost their ability to hear, and it was mainly from this that they devolved into a beast of burden—loyal to mankind, but still a burden bearer. But there was also a remnant that retained their ability, their sense of knowing. This remnant formed the lineage from which Avram and his herd had evolved.

It was in this knowing that Avram now stood. He maintained his guard on the top of the hill. From this position he could see all the herd. He lifted his head slightly, twitched his ears, and smelled the air as he listened for the Voice. Although He wasn't speaking, His presence was near.

It was time. Sasha was about to give birth. The only daughter out of his favourite mare, Rahkel, another Remnant, just like her mother before her, and her mother before that.

The Remnants were a special breed of horse, bred for the sole purpose of serving the King. They were equally suited for carriage and for riding. They were level-headed and measured in their interactions with people and their environment, making them an ideal horse for such a weighty responsibility. Breeds such as the warm blood, while making wonderful sporting and recreational horses, are not so suited for the regal responsibilities of belonging to the king's court.

It was an honour to be chosen to serve the King and to live in the royal mews. The mews was originally built to confine hawks and other birds of prey during their moulting season. Built in facing rows, and opening to a centre lane, they were later converted into stables, with housing above the stalls for coachmen and stable hands. Here, the horses were provided with fresh, sweet hay in abundance, a large stall with all the comforts a horse could ever want, and special treats from the hands of the Trainer.

Although Sasha had not been called into the Royal Stables for service, she was confident that, as a part of the Remnant, she would serve a particular purpose; she just didn't know what it was. She was content to wait. It would be revealed at the proper time.

Sasha had been in foal for eleven months. Although she was excited to be giving birth, and looked forward to her delivery, she was also content to let nature take its course. She had listened to the other mares as they spoke of her largeness, and she pondered their words. She had an instinctive knowledge that this foaling was different.

Sharing her concerns with Avram in the cool of the day, she said "Lately, I've felt as if two foals were inside of me. Do you think it's possible? What if there are two inside of me? The other mares have been saying how large my belly is. What do you think, Avram? Will they both survive? I don't think I could bear to lose a foal, not after carrying it for so long. Ooh, there it goes again. It's like there's two of them playing a game inside of me."

Avram laughed tenderly. "Hold on Sasha. You've asked me so many questions, I don't know which one to respond to first. I know the birth of two foals is an extremely rare event, but how about we leave that up to the Voice. Put your trust in Him. If you do have two foals within you, it is for a purpose.

And the King will take good care of you. You know that don't you?"

"Of course. It's just that I had forgotten. I don't know why. When I think of the Voice, I know that everything will be just as it ought. But, as the time gets closer, I sometimes forget to talk to the Voice. Is that bad?"

"Of course not. It's quite natural." Avram placed his head over the back of her neck in a comforting gesture until he felt her relax.

"The Voice is always with you, even when you don't feel His presence. He is all around us; He's in everything, and everything is for His purpose. It is important for you to remember that."

"Of course. I guess I'm nervous and excited at the same time."

Sasha felt reassured by the soft, comforting words of Avram and by his loving attention to her peace. As with every new mother, Sasha hoped and prayed that both foals, if two there were, would be born alive and that they would both survive. This, she knew, she would have to leave to the Voice.

Avram's gentle advice had reassured her. Now, as she reflected on their previous conversation, she drew on the strength that he had imparted. She had no time to think any more; her pains had started, and she was fully occupied in the birth process.

The Trainer, who had been watching her closely for days, had transferred her to the Royal stables only hours before. He was very tender toward her, and showed extreme care when he led her into the horse float. It didn't take long to be safely escorted into the birthing stall in the mews.

Sasha sniffed at the air and gave a cursory survey of her surroundings. There was no longer any evidence of the previous tenants, the king's hawks; they had been moved to a different residence and their housing had been converted into well-appointed stables. She didn't have much energy to waste on observations. That would have to come later as she was now fully occupied. She wondered, more by an inner sense than anything else, if she was living out her purpose—that this birth was her purpose in life. The answer to her silent questions would have to wait.

2. The Blessing

Avram watched as Sasha was taken away in the horse float. He stayed on, like a strong sentry, and waited in silence. The sun on his back, the soft breeze gently caressing his strong body, and the dragonflies hovering over the water in the stream below didn't distract him from his purpose. He was listening.

It would soon be time to pass on the blessing and Avram needed to hear it. Every time a Remnant was born, there was always a Blessing of Inheritance. Avram wanted to use his gift well, that of hearing the Voice.

Sasha had been taken to the Royal stables for the birth of her foal. She was placed in an overly large stall, with many birthing aids close by. Soft, warm hay carpeted the stall. A water bucket was placed within easy reach but there was no feed trough. Not that she minded the lack of feed; she would be too busy to eat, and hunger had departed from her many hours previously. There was a long rope hanging on a hook, another instrument used for hearing the heartbeat, a large suction tube and various other implements. In between contractions, she looked at these implements but could make no sense of them, so she turned her attention, instead, to the soft, warm hay.

As she lay in the birthing stall, she remembered all that her mother, Rahkel, had taught her. "As a Remnant, you have a special purpose in life that no one else can serve", she had said in her gentle and wise way. "Be content to wait. There is a time for everything." was another of her teachings. Sasha still wondered what her purpose was but was confident that, in time, it would be revealed. She was unaware that she was already living it in her foaling.

There was a buzz in the air as the stable horses listened to the foaling noises coming from the birthing stall at the far end of the stables. Their curiosity increased as they saw Avram making his way into the stables. Of all the horses in the field, he was the only one allowed to wander into the royal stables at will. Although put out to grass, he still carried the place of highest honour; he had been one of the six royal carriage horses, before his retirement, chosen for the inauguration ceremony of the current king. This was an honour among both men and horse and carried with it a special degree of privilege.

The foaling was progressing nicely and, before long, an energetic male was born. He didn't take long to find his legs and to stand. A few wobbles and a few uncertain steps and he was confident. He looked around with interest and stood firm, being quite pleased with himself. His onlookers were also pleased with him; he was the traditional grey colour with a slight silver sheen and his coat was already looking quite glossy, as if it had just been brushed for hours with a curry comb.

"Steady, girl," the Trainer said. He had passed the young foal on to a helper and had his attention focussed on Sasha again. "We're not quite finished, yet."

In a short space of time, another foal was born, just as grey and glossy, amid many surprised and awed onlookers. This was a very unusual occurrence and most of the onlookers were pessimistic about the chances of survival for the second foal. After all, horses weren't made to bear or to suckle more than one foal in normal circumstances. How on earth was this one going to survive?

He, also, was a good-looking male like his brother. He took longer to stand. He tried his front feet first; they seemed to work well. Then, he tried his back legs, but he couldn't seem to get them to stay under his body. They kept slipping out, sideways, and seemed to have a mind of their own.

He was also grey in colouring although a much lighter shade of grey, making him look as if he was silver in colour.

While a few of the onlookers began to whisper to each other under their breaths, mostly about how long this foal would last before he succumbed to his apparent weakness,

Avram came into view and took his place at the front of the crowd.

"Listen to the words of the Voice". Avram wasn't interested in what the local gossips were saying. He had a message to deliver, and he was focussed.

"You have wondered why your belly was so heavy," addressing himself to Sasha. *"You have wondered if all deliveries carried as much pain and discomfort as you experienced. By the Voice, you have been chosen and given an abundance. You carried within your belly two foals, both destined for a purpose, both chosen as Remnants. Only one will be destined for greatness. One will carry a harness; the other will carry freedom, but that freedom will come at a cost. One carries the excellency of dignity, majesty, and power, the other carries the beginning of strength. One bows his head to love and authority; the other has his head and his body bowed low."*

And then Avram walked away before he was bombarded with questions from the curious onlookers.

The Trainer looked at Avram with love in his eyes but it wasn't quite apparent whether or not he knew what had just happened.

"Did you hear that?" one of the onlookers said to no-one in particular.

One of the stable horses responded. "That was a strange Blessing. I've heard quite a few Blessings in my day, but none has been as enigmatic as that one. I wonder what it means."

A third by-stander piped up with, "In time, we'll know. These Blessings have a way of making known their meaning." And, at that, most of the horses seemed to be content.

There was a hush of awe over the brood as they digested the Blessing. What was the meaning of the words? Who could understand? The Blessing seemed to indicate that both foals would survive. That, in itself, was another miracle.

Then, all eyes turned toward Sasha to see what she would say about the Blessing but, if the mares thought they would have a comfortable gossip, they were sadly mistaken. If they thought that Sasha could, or would, shed light on the Blessing, they were also mistaken. It was a hard word to understand.

Seeing the stronger foal nuzzle into her, they left her to do her mothering in peace.

3. Wild and Free

*B*oth foals survived, which was as exciting as it was unusual. They were a perfectly matched pair of glossy, silver foals, growing stronger and stronger each day. After many days, even the one born second, who took a little time to find his legs, was looking as strong and as handsome as his older brother.

The oldest foal was named Keseph because his rich, silver coat reminded Sasha of an ancient word for silver. The youngest, whose coat was the same rich silver, also had a curious blaze on his forehead where the hair grew in a contrary direction, forming a cross-shaped pattern. It wasn't unusual for a horse to have a blaze on its forehead but, while most blazes were white, this one was different. His mother named him Argent, another ancient word meaning white or shining. Argentum, Sasha had heard, was often used in jewellery, coins and drinking vessels and was highly prized. Sasha rightly prized both of her new foals.

Keseph and Argent spent a lot of their time frolicking in the open field, running wild and free. The grass was soft and sweet, especially after the rain. The sky was clear; not a rain cloud in sight, and birds and butterflies buzzed in abundance. The sun was warm on their backs and the old Oak tree, where Avram spent most of his days, gave welcome relief to tired bodies.

The young ones had developed a strong bond between them. They often knew what the other was thinking. Indeed, they thought and acted as one for a large part of the time, giving such joy to Sasha.

One day, they were kicking up their heels in the field, close to where Avram was resting under his oak tree, when they noticed a carriage along the side of the road bordering the field. Keseph, always one to jump into action first, cantered to the fence line to inspect the carriage. Argent wasn't far behind but stood at a respectful distance.

Keseph called to the carriage horses. "Hello you lot. Come over and play with us. It's a great day for a romp in the field".

Argent was the one to notice the look of the carriage. It was edged in gold, with the most beautiful filigree. There were four golden lamp holders at each of the corners of the carriage to hold a light, the glass of which was etched with a pattern. The carriage was painted a glossy black with a huge crest on the door. Judging from the size of the crest, and the fact that some of the paint was gold, Argent thought the carriage must belong to a very important person, indeed.

There were six, large, dapple greys pulling the carriage. The livery, which included the harnesses and straps used to connect the horses with each other and with the carriage, stood out as royal: red, gold, and black. The horses carried golden bells on their feet that would chime with every movement. They also had pom poms on their head and along the length of their back with the same little, golden bells.

But, as the carriage pulled up on the road, there was not one tinkle, not one sound. The horses, although standing at complete ease, didn't make even the tiniest sound of their bells. Argent was intrigued. Then he noticed something else, or rather, someone else.

There was a man underneath the carriage! Did he know how dangerous that was? Obviously not! He was on his back, just behind the horses' heels, and seemed to be working on something between the horses and the carriage. Argent thought that, if one of the horses kicked or stepped back, the man could be killed. But he didn't seem to be afraid. Argent realised that he had complete confidence in each of the horses, and in their training. They were so disciplined. Argent was in awe of each of those horses, and in the man who could place his confidence, even his life, in his horses.

"Come and play with us", called Keseph a second time. "We have many great games to play. We can teach you. Come on".

But the horses didn't respond. They didn't even turn their heads to look. Keseph felt ignored. He didn't understand. He didn't notice the harnesses, or the bells on their feet or the pom poms on their heads. He was only interested in why they weren't eager to come and play.

"What's the matter? Are you too tired to come and play? he called.

Keseph was beginning to get a little annoyed. "Are you afraid? Aren't you strong enough?", he taunted.

Nothing. Not even a little quiver of their muscle. They didn't toss their head, neigh, or stamp their feet. They stood quite still, waiting for the voice of the Master.

Argent understood Keseph's desire to play. He also would have liked to play with them, but he sensed that they were different.

"Leave them, Keseph. I don't think they want to play," Argent said. But Keseph, who was getting quite annoyed that there was no response from any of them, continued.

"Why stand in the hot sun? That's not sensible. Come and stand in the shade of our oak tree. You can have a nibble on our sweet grass if you like. Aren't you hungry?"

Still not a word or a movement.

Keseph ran away in disgust and bewilderment. Argent followed soon after but not without a final glance at the man under the carriage and the horses who all stood in complete unison.

4. An Important Visitor

$\mathcal{T}$he man who was under the carriage stood up and came to stand by the fence. He was looking intently at the horses in the field. They were a good herd. Several foals had been born last spring and were almost ready to be put to service. After proudly surveying the herd, his eyes rested on Keseph and Argent.

The gossip amongst the herd was that one of the King's horses had retired and a replacement was being sought. Those of a dappled colouring were confident that one of them would be chosen. After all, they matched the horses already pulling the carriage. It made sense to choose another of the same.

Their excitement grew as the man looked over the herd. In the world of men, he was called the Trainer. It was his job to select and train horses for the royal stables. He was a gentle and patient man, full of wisdom and knowledge. He was seen talking to a second man, the Caretaker. This man was the one who came often to make sure the herd was well cared for, the grass was well watered, and the stream of water was still flowing.

Avram had recently felt a change in the air that he couldn't quite define. He had lately overheard a conversation between the Trainer and the Caretaker which sounded full of concern and seriousness, so he warned the young foals in the herd. "There may come times of hardship for us. The future seems to be a little uncertain. If you are chosen, make sure you conduct yourselves with wisdom, grace, and humility," he said. But, in their youth, most of his words fell on deaf ears. Their senses were not attuned to anything outside of themselves and their environment, yet.

Several of the horses were inspected more closely. The Trainer and the Caretaker came with a large horse float. The foals' excitement was growing. Each one hoped to be the one chosen. They knew what an honour it was to be chosen; they had listened often enough to the stories Avram had told. But, to their disappointment, both men walked over to Keseph and Argent.

The Trainer took his time with these two, trying to decide between the two. Both had wide, deep chests to accommodate a strong heart and a large lung capacity which was important in carriage pulling. They both had well-defined withers, short backs, and a deep girth. Most importantly, the Trainer looked at their hips, which were well rounded, and their powerfully defined muscles in their lower thighs. He looked them in the eyes; he ran his hands over their legs, feeling for muscle tone; and he spoke softly to them as he fondled them. They responded to this gentle treatment by nuzzling into his hand. What was that? Apple? What a wonderful treat. This man had their heart.

"I can't decide between the two," he said to the Caretaker. "What have you seen in these two?"

The Caretaker took his time before he responded. "This one", pointing to Keseph, "was strong and lusty as a newborn. He took to his mother within minutes of being born and was quite firm on his legs from the beginning. The other one", rubbing his hand on Argent's muzzle, "was a bit slower to get going but hasn't looked back. He has a strong will; he's very determined. Both of them, although they still frolic without a care in the world, seem to be very level-headed. I couldn't choose between them."

Again, more thoughtful silence, during which time the Trainer looked more intently into each one's eyes, as if looking into their soul. "I'll take them both", he said decidedly, and the deed was done.

Then, quite unexpectedly, a rope fell about the necks of both horses, and they were led off to the float. There was a bit of shinnying and a bit of kicking their heels as neither of them had been caught in such a fashion before. The only touch they had experienced in their short life was when the Caretaker came to feed them. He would hold out his hand and have some especially sweet feed for them to nibble. Or he would have an apple hidden in his pocket. They could always smell it, of course, but the Caretaker was encouraging them to come close, to build trust in them.

A filly was also chosen. She was roped and led toward the carriage in the same inglorious manner as Keseph and Argent, but with much less fuss on her part. She was out of a bay mother by Avram but, as a yearling, she appeared a lighter shade of golden wheat than her mother. The filly, who had every chance of taking on her mother's deeper gold as she matured, had glorious lines, was placid and well mannered—a perfect reflection of the legendary Remnants. Her name, Sheba, exactly suited her as she displayed a regal and gracious bearing. She wasn't proud in a disagreeable sort of way but there was something in the way she carried herself that showed she was destined for greatness.

"See that," one of the greys had said. "Sheba has been chosen, as well."

"Why her?" someone questioned.

"Why not? She's probably one of the prettiest fillies in the herd. And she always has that special look about her", the first one responded.

"Oh, I know. I guess she deserves it, but I wish I was chosen as well."

The other dapples were both excited and envious; excited that one of their lineage was chosen but envious that it wasn't one of them. They knew the honour that was given to anyone who was chosen for the King's stables. Wasn't their field next to the one used for retired horses from the royal stables? Didn't they learn some of the things that went on in the royal household from the retired horses? Not that they were given to gossip. The retired horses from the royal stables knew how to hold their tongues (as the saying was!). They never gave away any information of a private nature but only of a general nature as to the running of the royal stables and the conditions there. They knew, for instance, of the complete luxury of each of the stalls. Every horse had its own stall filled with soft, warm straw; there was food and water in abundance; and a daily brushing until their coats shone with gloss. Frequently inspected, they were in top physical condition and lacked nothing—not even the occasional apple treat that the Trainer had brought with him on his visit to the field when he inspected the herd.

Keseph, Argent and Sheba were a little unsettled in the float as they travelled along the road. They were experiencing a jumble of conflicting emotions.

"I wonder what will happen to us," Sheba whispered. "Are you scared, Argent?"

"Mmmm. I don't think I'm scared, exactly, but I'll miss my mother and the rest of the herd. I wonder if we'll be back," he replied.

"This is an adventure," said Keseph. "Aren't you just a little bit excited?"

"I wonder what we'll really be doing," said Sheba.

"Who cares? Think of all that glorious food. And the apple treats. It's going to be great. I just know it." Keseph was full of confidence.

He knew they would have plenty of food and water in the royal stables because he had heard from the retired horses of the plenteous provision of the King. But Argent was more curious about what they would be doing. The retired horses were quite silent on their previous activities.

After a moment of silence, Keseph spoke up again.

"I don't care what we have to do," he said, "because we're going to live in the royal stables. Do you know how important that is? I mean, we've been chosen above all the other horses."

Sheba responded, "You mustn't think more about the glory or the honour that will be ours. After all, we're not any more important than the King himself."

This comment put a damper on the conversation. It seemed to put their curiosity back into proper perspective.

Argent was quiet, thinking about what was left behind and wondering about what was in store. He decided, agreeing with all that Sheba had said, that the reason behind them being chosen might have more to do with service than with honour or glory. He tried to say as much to Keseph and Sheba, but Keseph was already thinking of how much he was going to enjoy his new life.

Keseph was thinking of the Blessing that had been spoken over him at his birth which his mother had faithfully repeated to him until he knew it word for word. The same words were, of course, spoken over his twin but, as Keseph was the eldest, he had the first right to the inheritance of the Blessing. This was the Remnant way.

Argent could also recite the Blessing word for word, but he wasn't thinking of this. He was thinking of the King. Luxury was all very well, but what was the point of living in luxury if the King wasn't a good king! They hadn't heard anything about the King, but they had seen the Trainer.

Argent was thinking of the Trainer, who he had later recognised as the one to lay beneath the horses. He was thinking of how, when the carriage stopped, the Trainer was confident enough to lay under the trace, between the horses, right next to their hooves where he could have been trodden upon. What sort of man does that? Was that a reflection on the man himself, or was it a reflection on the King? While Sheba was content to find out about the royal stables when she got there, Argent was feeling a stirring deep inside, as if something momentous was about to happen.

5. A New Day Dawns

After a short while, the trio noticed that the familiar countryside images were gradually decreasing as they came closer and closer to civilisation. None of them had been outside of their own countryside before. They weren't aware that the King, although owning all the country, had set aside a particular part of the countryside for the breeding and rearing of his horses. He had seen the value of the land, with its lush grass and constant, fresh water supply, as a place for his herd.

The herd was quite extensive. Here, horses were bred for all sorts of uses. Some were used to pull farming implements (for the King fed a great many people); some were used for the entertainment of children on special occasions; and a few were chosen for the special use of the King in his royal stables. But all were looked after and kept in top condition. All were bred from the best lines around the world; all developed fine, muscular bodies, fit for purpose, throughout their lives.

"Have you noticed that there are more cottages as we pass by?" asked Argent to no one in particular. There was washing on the lines and farmers working their fields. There were people pulling wagons and carts along the same road, always giving way to the carriage.

"Yes, but there's less grass," said Sheba. "I wonder where people run?"

The road upon which they were travelling was a dirt road, well maintained, with grass on the sides of the road. Buttercups grew in the fields on each side, occasionally laced with lavender coloured flowers that the horses had not seen before.

"Look," said Sheba. "They have the same flowers here that we have in our countryside, you know, the bright yellow ones. I wonder why they only grow around the cottages in those strips of dirt instead of all over." She wasn't sure what she thought about that!

Gradually, the dirt road blended into a road that was paved with cobblestones. Travelling over this part of the road was a bit bumpy and a little unpleasant.

"If we have to travel for too much longer on these stones, we'll get shaken to pieces," Keseph complained.

"Mmmm," said Sheba distractedly.

Keseph wasn't certain if she agreed, or not.

Arriving at their destination, they were let in through two huge iron gates that had to be opened by two well-dressed gatemen. The gates, and the wall in which they were situated, kept out anyone who did not have business with the King or people of his court.

Immediately inside the gates, there was a great courtyard full of all sorts of people, buying and selling from stalls around the edges of the courtyard. There were minstrels playing on musical instruments, walking around singing and telling funny stories. Brightly coloured flags and banners flew in the soft breeze with the King's standard topping them all. It was flown quite high over all the palace, from a pole located on the top of the roof.

All three horses looked around with such interest, having a hard time taking in all the happy sights and sounds. Each of them felt a sense of wonderment and awe at the richness of all that they saw. This had the effect of, temporarily, making Keseph forget his jolted body.

Eventually, they were led off to an area on the eastern side of the palace. The buildings were made of cut stones, regular in shape, well insulated against the weather. Some had doors of solid oak; some had no doors but only a large opening as an entryway. They were all paved with the same stones as on the road. Although the stones were worn smooth in most places, Keseph was not impressed!

The horses were unloaded from the float and led into large, well-equipped stalls. They were all kept together, their stalls being next to each other's. This gave them the opportunity to continue speaking and to be less homesick as they were more familiar with each other than their new surroundings.

"Argent, did you notice that, while we were being led into our stalls, the horses pulling our float stood still: They didn't even move a muscle!"

"I did, Sheba. I wonder how they do that?" replied Argent.

Keseph didn't notice and was even less interested. He was looking out the window of his stall, observing his surroundings and resting, the tip of his rear left hoof just touching the ground. He was enjoying the lack of jostling and the comfort of his new stall.

"I've been wondering why we were chosen, Argent," Sheba said. "What job do you think we'll be given?"

"I don't know. I've been wondering that myself," Argent replied, "but I think we just need to wait. Perhaps we'll find out tomorrow."

Keseph chipped in, "Well, I for one, haven't forgotten the prophecy. We were born for greatness. It should be obvious why we were chosen, Argent, but I'm not sure about Sheba—unless you had a similar prophecy when you were born?"

"Not that I can remember," she replied.

Argent looked around his stall with interest, recognising some familar smells and wondering about other, less familar ones. He noticed the comfort, but he was too interested in the things that lined his stall. On one wall was an arrangement of bridles, halters, bits, and other things that he had never seen before. He was lost in his imagination, wondering what each of them might be doing there and what was their purpose. Sheba interrupted his thoughts.

"Look, Argent," said Sheba. "Can you see that yard out there to the south? Can you see what those horses are doing?"

Argent's attention turned in the direction Sheba was looking, and he saw what had caught her eye. There was another horse running in circles around the outside of a yard. They both thought that was strange behaviour. If he wanted to run, why didn't he just go out into the field, like other horses, and run wild and free?

There was so much they wanted to know about their new surroundings and what they would be doing in the King's stables but none of their questions would be answered until the morrow. Argent and Sheba decided it would be best to follow Keseph's lead and rest, so they stood, one leg raised, and began nibbling on the feed so generously provided, and waited for the new day to dawn.

6. Training Begins

Their new surroundings were encouraging. The stall was quite spacious and the feed, delivered twice a day by a well-dressed man, was fresh and generous. In the morning light, they had time to fully observe what lay beyond their stalls. They could see the yard that Sheba noticed the previous night and several other yards beyond that one. They were not impressed. Each of the yards was covered in brown dirt and bordered by fences—lots of dirt; lots of fences. None of the trio were happy to leave their herd, their mother, or the soft, green fields of what had been the only home they knew, even though they appreciated the comfort of their stall.

In the early light of the new day, the well-dressed man who brought them their food, came to visit each of them. In time, even though they had seen him before, they learned he was called the Trainer. He looked around the stall; looked over each of them, feeling their legs; running his hand down their bodies and, finally, their noses. He spoke kindly and gently to each of them. While his language was new to them, it didn't take long before they began to understand a lot of the words he used. He was calling them "beautiful", "my lovely", and "chosen". He was making sure that they were rested, and that they hadn't experienced any trouble from their journey to the royal stables, the mews.

Satisfied with what he had seen of the horses, he led them out to one of the yards they had seen from their stalls. Over his shoulder, he called instructions to a younger man standing close by. This seemed to cause a flurry of activity in the stables but, as the horses were unused to the daily routine, they weren't in the least bit interested in what those instructions were.

The yard they were led into was the largest of the yards that they could see. It was bounded by four, straight fences, and had one or two other men standing up on the fence to see them as they entered the yard. Sheba watched them as she ran into the centre of the yard. They were talking amongst themselves and pointing to the horses from time to time. Sheba thought she recognised appreciation on their faces but couldn't be sure.

"What are they staring at, Argent?" Sheba asked Keseph. As Keseph and Argent ran in faster than she did, they were totally unaware of the other men, ready to explore their new space and run the fidgets out of their legs. Eventually, Keseph said he didn't care but Argent was a little more interested, having had them pointed out to him.

"I'm not sure, but they don't look like they mean us any harm," Argent said.

The Trainer had provided a couple of very large balls for them to play with. Keseph and Argent thoroughly enjoyed investigating these balls, pushing them with their noses, then chasing them around the yard. They ran over to Sheba and invited her to play along with them. She joined in but it was hard to run as the space was much smaller than their spacious fields at home.

Home? Where was that? Sheba wondered if they would ever return to their home in the fields or if this was to be their new home forever. She began to feel a little homesick but, as Keseph came back at her with his playful nature, she was diverted from her thoughts and continued to play, as best she could.

After the novelty of the balls wore off, one by one they began to experience a sense of being closed in, even though they were outside. Sheba was the first to stop playing. She stood still, looking toward the east as if trying to see beyond the other yards.

"Hey, Sheba. What's up?" asked Argent. Keseph came over to them and joined the conversation.

"I was just trying to see if I could see home," she said. "I think our fields were over there but it's too hard to tell. So much has happened since we left home and I'm not sure we'll ever see it again."

"Home was good, but this place is good, too," said Keseph. "We have all the food we want; our stalls are really quite luxurious; we have this yard with its balls to play in; and the Trainer is a really nice, gentle man. What else could we possibly want?" But even as he said this, Keseph was aware of a very small emptiness inside of him.

"It's the fences," Argent said as he looked around. "I know we had fences at home, but they were so much further apart. They stopped us from going into that dry area where there was little grass and water. These ones are so…"

"And the dirt," said Sheba.

The trio remembered the grass they had to play on, and the fences were so far away that they didn't stop them from running wild and free. "How I miss running up and down those gentle hills," Sheba said wistfully, more to herself than to Keseph or Argent.

They all stood silently for a while, lost in their own thoughts. Then, one by one, they ran from fence to fence, looking for a way out, suddenly realising the truth of their confinement. They were stuck! All interest in the balls was forgotten. What was this place? What had they done to deserve this?

Sometime later, they were escorted back to their stalls. There was fresh hay in the stalls, the food bucket had been filled again, and fresh water was in another bucket, but this extravagant supply was lost on them. They were homesick.

The Trainer came again to speak with each of them. He had such a soothing voice and such a caring manner. It helped them with their homesickness but didn't take it away. Sheba was the first to respond to his gentleness.

"I like the Trainer. He seems to understand how I feel. I didn't understand his words but there was something in his tone, something in his eyes, and in how he spoke to me," she said. Keseph and Argent didn't respond so she turned her attention to the feed bucket. Mmmm, it was good.

In the afternoon, a farrier came to visit. They needed to be prepared for the cobblestones streets on which they might be walking, and strong, steel shoes would be perfect for that.

"Oooh, I don't like the feel of these things on my feet," complained Keseph. "They're so heavy. They'll slow down our running."

"I don't mind them," said Argent, the first to be shod. "You get used to them after a while."

"Yesterday, I saw a couple of other horses further down in the stables and I noticed that they were wearing these things on their feet. I wondered what they were," Keseph said. "Now, I know."

They didn't realise it, but they were being prepared for training.

First, the lead line. Keseph had a lead line attached to his bridle and was taken out into the yard. He didn't mind it. The lead line was kept loose and, at first, he could walk wherever he wanted. Then, the Trainer began to lead him, first this direction, then the opposite direction. This went on for days, being led in a circle for no apparent reason. None of the trio knew for how many days but each became bored with the repetition.

Then the trainer changed things a little. He put a few obstacles in their way. One was a small tree trunk they had to walk over; another was a piece of material they had never seen before. It was held down in the corners so the wind wouldn't blow it away, and there was a large wooden plank placed over the top. They were expected to walk on top of the wooden plank. It wasn't hard, but it was unusual. Neither of them had seen anything like it before. They all managed the obstacles, and the Trainer was pleased with all three.

"Hey, Keseph," Sheba called from her stall, "How did you like today's games?"

"I didn't mind," he responded. It was fun. What about you?"

"I mostly liked it, but I wasn't sure about the big, wooden thing I had to walk over. It made a noise when the wind blew and scared me a little, but the Trainer was so encouraging."

"It didn't make a noise for me," said Argent, "but the broken tree that I had to step over was a bit hard. It reminded me of the Oak tree that Avram stands under, you know, the one on top of the hill back home."

"No. This one was much smaller. Avram's tree is huge," replied Keseph.

"I know, but it wasn't the size that reminded me. Have you noticed that we don't have any trees here?"

"Yes, I've noticed," said Sheba, "but we have plenty of shade in the stables."

Trees or no trees, training continued. They learned to walk in the direction of the Trainer, at a gentle prompt from his hand; they crossed bridges, walked over fallen trees, walked over tarps on the ground, walked through narrow openings between bushes, up and down, over and across. They became quite good at leading. They learned to recognise even the gentlest of pressures given by the Trainer. This was one of the main ways he communicated with them, although he also taught them some strategic words.

After each short training session, they were led into their stalls where they were groomed by their own groomer. Their feet were cleaned to make sure they hadn't picked up any stones that would lead to lameness and pain. They were brushed from top to bottom until their coat shone.

"I love being brushed down after the training," Sheba said. I sound like the mares back home, she thought to herself.

"Me too. It's so therapeutic," Keseph replied.

This regime went on for days and weeks and the young horses felt so good. Home was beginning to be a thing of the past as they developed trust, acceptance, and responsiveness. Life was good.

But life, as they knew it, was about the change.

7. Disaster

All three horses were quick to learn the basics of leading and desensitisation. Not that they understood the 'why' of their training. They learned to lean away from the pressure of the Trainer instead of into the pressure, as their natural inclination was. This, of course, made them very responsive to the physical commands of the Trainer and set them up to be obedient to the verbal commands, a thing that was very important to the Trainer. They were also responsive to him when he was leading, long lining, or ground driving, impressing him with their progress and their willingness to learn.

The next morning, more intensive training began. They were taken out to the same yard again, one by one, but where they were used to spending fifteen minutes each in the round yard with the Trainer, they were now asked to run for longer and longer periods. 'Asked' is not exactly the right word; they were forced to run.

First, their legs were dressed in protective wraps while in their stalls. Then, they were tacked up with saddle and bridle, or with bridle and long lines, one on either side, passing over their flanks and hindquarters. This heavier equipment took a little getting used to.

They were asked to walk on, trot, slow down and halt at the verbal commands they had learned earlier, all while learning to feel comfortable with the long lines touching their body.

As their training periods were getting longer and longer, they had less chance to talk with each other as they did before.

It wasn't until the end of the day, when they had been returned to the stalls, that had a chance to speak, but they were often so tired they didn't even bother.

At first, Keseph didn't mind. Once he got used to the feeling of the lines against his body, it was an easy thing to respond to the commands of the Trainer. Argent, also, was responsive to the Trainer as he stood behind, but slightly to the centre of the round yard. Sometimes the pressure on the line would change from right to left, or from left to right, and each horse would change movement in the direction the Trainer indicated with his pressure. They had learned to do this from their initial training.

Sheba's training was a little different. She had wondered if the change in her training had had anything to do with a lady that came to visit her in the stall late one afternoon, several days before. She seemed to be no ordinary lady. She was dressed in a riding habit of rich red and black velvet, sporting a black riding hat with a very large feather waving in the breeze as she moved. Not that Sheba knew anything about velvets or feathers but, from the number of people attending to her every need, Sheba judged her to be a very important member of the royal household.

She voiced her reasoning to Keseph and Argent that night. "Do you think I'll be doing something different now?" she asked them. "I think she must be a grand lady. She's obviously very important, but I don't know who she is".

"I would think so," said Argent. "You're training has changed. You're not doing the same things as us, are you?"

"Undoubtedly," said Keseph. She seemed to have a particular interest in you. She didn't spend more than a few seconds looking at me, and probably not at Argent, as well," said Keseph with a little jealousy.

The lady took great interest in Sheba, her stature, muscular tone, and overall beauty. She also watched Sheba's basic moves, walking, trotting, and cantering, in both straight lines and circles, and how she executed basic upward and downward transitions. She watched for how correct each movement was but also for consistency in each movement; every movement had to be exact every time. She seemed to be well pleased with all of Sheba's moves. She also spoke to Sheba, looking in her eyes, and Sheba felt a connection to the lady. It was only later, through the gossip chain of the other horses in the stable, that Sheba learned that the lady was none other than the King's wife—the Queen.

"Doesn't that make you feel important?" Keseph asked. "If I had the Queen showing special interest in me, I think I would. I mean, it's not everyone that is chosen by the Queen."

"I've not been chosen for anything, yet" Sheba said a little shyly.

"Yes, but I'm sure you will be," said Argent.

Mmmm, thought Sheba. Argent broke into their thoughts.

"You don't sound convinced, Sheba. What's on your mind?" he asked.

"Don't laugh," she said, taking her time to respond and lowering her voice so that the other horses didn't overhear. After the encouragement she saw in Argent's eyes, she felt as if he might understand. "I was wondering about my muscle tone."

Sheba wasn't game enough to give any more information than that. She thought she might just let that bit of information slip out, so to speak, and see what Argent said before she unburdened herself anymore.

"I like your muscle tone," Argent said with a hint of appreciation. He liked to see mares with good muscle tone because it meant, for him, that they had worked hard on the exercises and training regime. This showed character, a thing that Argent was more interested in than just physical beauty. "After all, Sheba, you could be the best-looking horse in the stables, or in the whole world, but if you get winded at the first hill, or if you can't stay the distance when you're working for an owner, what good are you?" he explained.

Argent's response reassured Sheba. She was secretly worried about having so much muscle tone, thinking it took away from her beauty as a mare, But Argent's perspective was encouraging. Sheba didn't want to pay as much attention to her looks as some of the other mares back home, thinking that a gentle heart was more important, but it was hard to not be influenced by others.

Was it sheer coincidence that Keseph made mention of their developing muscle tone the next morning? "Hey, Argent" he called. "Have you noticed anything about me lately? And you, too."

When Argent looked a bit mystified, Keseph prompted him. "Look at your flanks, brother."

Argent looked around, taking in his strong lines, but didn't comment.

"Look at your muscle tone, silly. Have you noticed how well-defined our bodies are looking? Even Sheba. It must be all the exercise we're doing."

"I don't think I've had time to even think about it," Argent said. "When I return to my stall, all I want to do is rest."

Keseph and Argent both liked running, but there was a lot more running nowadays. Training sessions were increased in time, frequency and duration. They were now doing ground driving to prepare them for taking a carriage. Verbal cues were hardly ever used; they got all the signals they needed from the line pressure. A lunging whip was also used, softly at first, along their hips. Once or twice, Keseph felt the whip a little more strongly but not in actual pain. The fun of running was slowly and very surely slipping away, being replaced by a very persistent and repetitive focus on the action of running.

Argent was just as tired as Keseph, and just as confused. He was tired of running. Who would have thought that his favourite game back in the field was now a torture? This new life was more like death! He couldn't understand what crime either of them had committed to deserve such a change in their circumstances. All he knew was that the process they were now going through was the most horrible thing they had ever known.

They both had to get used to a leather strap being placed around their girth and over their ribs. At first, it felt rather heavy but, gradually, they both got used to the weight of the girth strap. More straps were added to the girth strap, then a shaft was added to their sides. When they got used to the solid wooden shaft, a rubber tyre was attached to the shaft. They had to get used to the ever-increasing weight of all the added paraphernalia, called 'tack' by the stable hands. First it was one carriage wheel, then two, then three. The extra weight was hard to bear. New noises were also experienced and there was a different feeling in the whole movement as the weights moved from side to side around the round yard.

Days turned into weeks; weeks turned into months. The gruelling days of training were repeated over and over without a break. Both horses hated the crack of the whip which was used to help them get used to noises. The long line wasn't so bad, but the process was the same: round and around this way, halt, step backward, turn, round and around that way, all at the whim of the Trainer and with the extra weight to carry on the back of the long line. Again, they were not to know the reason behind his whims. All they knew was the monotony of training.

Every day was a 'head down tail up' sort of day. Every night was a welcome relief from the repetition of training but, if they cared to admit it, they were well looked after. All they thought about, in the days of their intensive training, was the great torture to which they had been subjected.

"What was our crime for this horrible existence?" Keseph moaned one night. Argent couldn't answer. Not only because he didn't have the answer but also because he didn't have the strength. Argent was still clinging to the idea that there was a purpose, somewhere, in all of this. He didn't associate his training with any crime. How could he? They were, all three, innocent of any crime, except perhaps that of enjoying life and freedom.

As if reading Argent's thoughts, Keseph continued, "Where has our freedom gone". "Do you remember the smell of the grass after it rained? And the butterflies that danced over the buttercups?"

With an effort, Argent replied. "Our stall is nice and warm. We must take comfort in that. And we get plenty of hay and oats". But even Argent was having a hard time being encouraged by his own words. He was just plain tired!

Argent was pondering Keseph's words, and all that had happened to them so far. The Trainer was a kindly, old man and both horses were progressing nicely with their training, benefiting from the continual running around the round yard. They were both building muscle and stamina as they ran. But, unknown to Argent, Keseph was also pondering. But what he saw was totally different. He saw the endless training, the brown dirt of the yards, and the intense, purposeful walking, trotting, and cantering instead of the unrestrained enthusiasm he had back home in his field.

"This is too much," Keseph decided one day. There were now four carriage wheels on the back of the line and still he was expected to trot in circles in the round yard. While the Trainer was asking for a trot, Keseph yearned for a run on the hills of his homeland. He wanted to be free, just once, and then he could continue with his training, he thought.

Keseph lost focus and imagined himself on the hills and meadows of his home and, forgetting where he was for just a moment, broke out of the trot and began to run, straining the tendons in his legs. Suddenly, he felt the intense pain—like his knee was on fire—and he stumbled forward. The Trainer was quick to see what had happened and, very lovingly, came to his rescue. But the damage to his tendon had been done.

The Trainer carefully led Keseph back to his stall, giving urgent directions to the stable boys nearby, speaking soothingly to Keseph. But something happened in Keseph's heart that couldn't be mended with soothing words, poultices or any other medicinal aid.

8. Heart's Response

While Keseph's knee healed, training for Argent continued. Keseph had the rest for which he longed and came back to training with renewed energy, but his heart wasn't in it as it was before. The Trainer sensed the change in Keseph but put it down to the strain he had received. He wasn't as exacting with Keseph, assuming that his heart would, once more, be engaged.

Lunging allowed the young horses to burn off their extra energy. At any given moment, and at a randomly selected time-period, the Trainer would change direction. This increased their balance and their flexibility, but this was known only to the Trainer. The two horses were quite oblivious to the benefits of lunging. All they saw was the repetition and hard work. Even Argent was beginning to question his existence.

Then the lunging was followed up with two lines as the horses continued their training in carriage work. They were trained to hear a repetitious noise, like the jingle of the tack, or a sudden, threatening noise like a car horn or dog bark, and not react out of fear. While many trainers used whips and a variety of other aids for control, the Trainer only used his hand signals and his voice to control the horses, so their obedience was dependent on these two methods of control.

They also continued their ground driving. Still in the round yard, they were expected to pull the shafts of a cart in a walk or trot, all while the Trainer walked behind, slightly to the inside of the horse. No more running. Their joy at running was being curtailed.

They no longer saw much of Sheba. She had been moved to a different stall and her training, although just as rigorous, followed a different pattern. Neither Keseph, nor Argent, had much time for wondering how she was getting on with her training. She was being trained for the dual purpose of carrying her Queen in riding exercises and for pulling her phaeton. Her gentle heart and willing spirit made her a fit choice for the Queen's various needs.

Like Argent, Keseph was showing great promise as his muscles developed. He was strong and sturdy and would be a great asset to the Master. But ever since his tendon strain, Keseph was a little slower than Argent to respond to the discipline of the ground driving. Did he not see the clues, as Argent had done? This slowness was not missed by the Trainer.

The Trainer also used a particular tone of voice when lunging and when driving. He was stern, without being cross or mean; he was direct and clear with his instructions. Argent began to understand 'walk', 'trot' and 'canter' as separate and distinct words. Keseph understood the long, drawn out 'whoooaaa'. But, again, he wasn't as quick to respond to the words that Argent was beginning to understand.

The Trainer was always taking good care of his horses, even during a rigorous training program. One morning, during the early days of their confinement, the Trainer came into the stalls with special, protective wraps for their lower legs. The wraps added compression to their legs to help reinforce their muscles. With these wraps on their legs, they would be less likely to sustain an injury. He spoke soothingly to both as he placed the wraps over their fetlocks and cannon bones. He knew they needed extra protection on this part of their legs during the repetitious training exercises. While the wraps felt strange at first, when training time came both Argent and Keseph could feel the extra protection on their legs and were grateful for the extra care.

As the training continued, the Trainer was getting a good feel for both horses. He loved them both, very dearly, but could see that Argent was responding quicker than Keseph. The Trainer knew that, for some reason, he wasn't getting to the heart of Keseph. Keseph did everything that was asked of him, his muscles were developing and showing good definition in his body, and his balance and flexibility were increasing. But there was something holding him back. In the transitions, the changing from walk to canter or from canter to gallop, he was just a second or so slower to respond than Argent. Keseph sometimes reacted, ever so slightly, to sudden noises. For some reason, he was particularly put off by the sound of a dog barking.

Argent, on the other hand, was quick to learn and quick to respond. He could detect the Trainer's change of tone when he spoke to either of the horses. He could also see and feel the loving way his hands worked over his body as he inspected his muscles for any signs of fatigue or injury. The training was tough. They were expected to be as obedient when being led as they were when on the lunge line or in harness.

The Trainer had taken to just walking them into the round yard with the halter and turning his back to them. Argent responded immediately. He didn't like the feeling of rejection that came over him whenever the Trainer's back was turned and came to nuzzle up to the Trainer for affirmation. He always got a reward. Sometimes a carrot, sometimes a juicy, red apple. Keseph didn't like it either. He wondered why he wasn't being trained. Why wasn't he the focus of the Trainer's attention as he had once been? He felt as if he was being overlooked but eventually sought the Trainer for reassurance.

That night, Keseph made a decision. He wasn't sure how he was going to accomplish it, but he determined that he would—somehow.

"Argent", Keseph whispered, "Do you ever think about our old home? Do you remember the hills and how we used to run and frolic and go wherever we wanted? Do you ever think of the sweet smell of the grass after rain? I miss the taste of the grass. And I miss being able to run wherever and whenever I want."

Argent didn't respond immediately. He, too, was remembering but he also recognized his memory as the pointless meanderings of nostalgia and was about to say something when Keseph stamped his feet and gave a short whinny.

"We were both born for greatness. Where is our greatness here? It's just daily toil." Thinking of the words of the Blessing, he said "I don't think this is my purpose in life."

"But Keseph, we're being trained for something great. Don't you feel it? And the Trainer loves us both very much". Argent was torn. While he fondly remembered his early days in the field, he also valued the training and, for the first time, realised that he loved the Trainer more than his previous life. He began to ask himself, "Was he finally at home in this place of brown?". He thought longingly of the sweet, fresh water of the stream and of his herd. He missed his mother and the other mares. He missed seeing Avram standing tall and proud on the hill, his glossy, black coat shining in the sun. Argent was no longer torn—he belonged to the King, wholeheartedly.

Wakened from his thoughts, he heard the voice of Keseph.

"I've made a decision", Keseph said with finality. "At the first sign of freedom, I'm going to take it. I'm not staying here any longer than I have to. You can come, too. Yes. Do come. We'll go back to where we were truly happy and…"

"But, Keseph, I'm happy here. If I left, I would miss our dear Trainer."

"Oh, what do you know about anything? As your older brother, I could order you to come."

"By less than half an hour" Argent added half under his breath.

Keseph had nothing more to say.

9. Now or Never

The next morning, and much earlier than Keseph had expected, an opportunity came for him to escape. At first, he wondered why his escape opportunity was so easy. But, determined to escape, he didn't dwell on the reason for the opportunity for too long. He knew it was a 'now or never' moment. He wasn't going to take any more of his confinement. He longed for the flowing streams of fresh water, his green hills, and his freedom.

He was surprised that he hadn't seen before how easy it would be to simply jump the fence and run along the road until he came to the tree line where he would be out of sight. "Why haven't I noticed this before?", he said to himself.

"I can't take any more of this confinement". Looking around for a response, he wondered, "Did I say that aloud?" Not bothering to wait for the answer, or to think through the consequences, he acted quickly.

Without looking to see if anyone was watching, he cantered a little distance from the fence line and then, picking up the pace, he ran with all his might toward the fence. He hadn't learned much about jumping in his training, so his fetlocks weren't used to the jarring of a landing on solid earth. "How hard could it be, anyway?", he reasoned with himself. It wasn't really a requirement of the Trainer or of being a carriage horse, he supposed, but that didn't stop him. Undaunted, he cleared the fence with sheer will power and the strength of his fine body.

If he was able to look at himself, he would have realized that he had developed into a champion. His legs were heavily muscled, for strength; his lower legs able to hold his weight and act as a springboard. This was crucial as he jumped the fence but, again, he was totally unaware of the importance of his physique. He had developed a deep, muscular torso, a long, thick neck and a regal head. These were essential characteristics of a horse that was designed for great things!

A little way down the road, he turned back to see if he was being followed. No. Nothing. No one.

Argent was watching Keseph's escape, sad for his future, but not knowing quite why. As Keseph was positioning himself to jump the fence, Argent looked around, his heart in his throat, to see if anyone else was watching. He thought he heard a sound coming from the stables and was in fear of what would happen to Keseph if he was caught, but Keseph cleared the fence easily and made a clean get away.

Turning back to the stables, after he saw Keseph make a clean jump of the fence, Argent saw the Trainer watching from the stables. He was astonished that the Trainer didn't go after Keseph. He just stood, motionless, watching Keseph first, and then Argent to see if he would follow. When he saw that Argent remained, he silently turned all his attention toward Argent. If Argent was in the stable, he would have been close enough to see the tears of regret and heartache that freely ran down the cheeks of the Trainer. He might have picked up on the agony of soul the Trainer was experiencing. Instead, Argent was standing in the yard, still amazed at what had just happened; amazed that Keseph had gone; amazed that the Trainer hadn't stopped him; and missing his brother with all his life.

At the end of the most bizarre day Argent had yet experienced, the Trainer was talking softly and tenderly to Argent as he groomed him. There was still the hint of a tear in the Trainer's eyes, but he kept talking softly and caressing Argent as he groomed him.

During all of this, Argent had time to think. He had no-one to whom he could talk anymore. He had a lot to think about. For instance, was it always that easy to escape by jumping the fence? It was strange that neither of them had noticed how low the fence was. Then there was the Trainer. Why didn't he go after Keseph? Didn't he want Keseph? Did he even like Keseph? Well, of course he wanted Keseph, and he liked

Keseph as much as he liked himself. Argent saw how tender he was toward Keseph. You can't be tender toward someone you don't like!

And most importantly, why didn't he go with Keseph? Why did he stay? He knew how hard the training was. Argent didn't expect the training to ease up just because Keseph had found his freedom. Then, as if struck by a bolt of lightning, Argent realized he actually enjoyed the training, and he loved the Trainer with such a deep love that he hadn't experienced before—not even for his mother, although it was a different type of love.

While the training got harder and harder, Argent applied himself in a way that he hadn't in the past. He was rapidly learning to submit even his own will, and to learn the ways of the Trainer. In fact, he now saw the Trainer as Master. This submission was resulting in a wisdom beyond himself. In response to the love of the Trainer, Argent was able to respond to the slightest wish of the Master, to the quietness in his voice and even to a look in his eyes, originating out of his own love toward the Master. This Wisdom told him that, had there been no testing in the form of a low fence, had Keseph not escaped and shown him how easy it was, there would not have been an opportunity for him to choose between submission and freedom. He also would not have realized how much love he had for the Master and what a profound effect this love had on him. This love, of course, grew out of the Master's love for himself—and Keseph.

Argent began to feel sorry for Keseph. As he was musing, he realised Keseph would never know the power of choice; he would never know the truth of sacrificial love; and he would never know the rebellion that lay in his heart until he was confronted with the opportunity to choose. In the sunny, carefree days of their home field, there was no need to rebel or submit; they were sinless in their innocence. When brought to the place of training, testing and discipline, the obedience of one and the rebellion of the other was made manifest. Being trained and tested was a risky business. Without the confinement and the training, the rebellion would not have been discovered. But then neither would have been the submission. Argent saw that, while he was tested, he was found to be mature. He was reflecting the characteristics and traits of his Master, the Trainer.

10. The King is Coming

rgent's training continued relentlessly. As a horse that was new to carriage driving, he was placed with more experienced horses to learn the basics of movement. He learned how to be the rear horse, hitched to the carriage shaft, and not seeing where he was going. This helped him develop trust as he followed, quite blindly, the rump in front of him. He learned the front position, responding to the directions of the Trainer and pulling the horse behind him. And, most importantly, he learned to work as part of a team, either of four or six, in front and back positions, left and right positions, until he moved as one with the rest of the team.

Finally, his period of training was over. He no longer wanted to go home and join Keseph and his family, for that would be going back; he wanted to go forward.

Although a greater confinement was his reward for submission and obedience, he was also experiencing a greater love than he had known before.

One of his favourite treats was when he was taken to a different area within the mews, groomed with a softening shampoo, and dried and brushed until his coat shone like velvet. His mane and tail were plaited to suit his regal appearance, and all the metal fittings of his harness, being of shiny, golden brass, were polished to shine in the sunlight. From the other horses in his team, he learned that they would soon be stepping out with the King. Argent could hardly believe it. If it was true, what an honour it would be to be in the King's team.

Three days later, the team was placed in a soft leather harness, embellished with brass. There were brass bells sitting up high on the backstrap that tinkled as the horses moved. The team also had smaller, red pom-poms on their browbands and an embroidered face piece of red and gold on fine white leather. Even though there was no need for blinkers, because of the training they had received by the Trainer, blinkers were used as part of the regalia, displaying the royal emblem.

The carriage, although not the ornate state carriage used for coronations, was almost as impressive. Smaller and lighter, it was made of dark mahogany wood, polished until you could see your reflection in it. The glass windows of the carriage shone like crystal. At each of the four corners of the carriage, there were golden lanterns to light the way, encasing engraved crystal through which the flame shone. Golden filigree patterns on the carriage proclaimed the importance of its occupant. The royal emblem, painted on the sides of the doors, was in gold, red, blue, and white. The wheels, larger at the back, were well sprung and painted in gold.

In harness, the horses could only move when and where the Trainer directed. Unless the Trainer spoke, they stood completely still. They had worked together as a team so often that they knew each other's thoughts and were able to move, or stay, as one. Argent had discovered some while back that his sole purpose in life was to be in harness for the King. As a result, he would be in training every day just to prepare him for that task.

Back in the mews, there was a buzz of excitement. The King was coming. When Argent asked the more experienced horses what the King was like, they just smiled, with such a warm look in their eyes, and said "You'll see!"

Argent had had little chance to talk with Sheba as she was used often by the Queen. She was the Queen's favourite mount for riding in the park and for visiting people in the kingdom. Sheba was out almost every day and, when she wasn't out, she was being groomed or was resting. He longed to speak with her but had to content himself with his new friends, for he had formed a special bond with each of the other carriage horses.

When the time came, the Trainer walked into the stables. This wasn't unusual, but what was unusual was the way the Trainer was dressed. He wasn't wearing his usual, very practical livery. He was wearing a suit of white linen underneath a coat of red wool. The coat was extremely well made by a very select tailor and had seven gold buttons at the front and three gold buttons on each of the sleeves. It also carried silver embroidery on each of the lapels. "Wow, Look at the Trainer! He almost looks like he's the King," Argent said aloud to his carriage mates. The response to his comment, although he wasn't expecting anyone to respond, was a little snigger of amusement. Argent realised, with a pang of both guilt and surprise for not realising it before: the Trainer was the Master, the King. Quite naturally, Argent was humbled. He had been trained—by the King! He had been spoken to with such tenderness—by the King. He had looked into the eyes of—the King! He no longer carried regret for Keseph; Argent's full focus was now on the King.

11. The Cost of Freedom

Standing on his wobbly legs, parched from thirst, Keseph stood still, listening to the noise of a carriage coming down the road. When he had first returned to his fields, he was quite content, nibbling on the sparse grass, swiping flies with his tail, and stamping his foot when they annoyed him. The stream of clear, fresh water that existed in his memory was no longer flowing as freely. He also had to move around the field constantly, looking for suitable feed as most of it was too hard and dry to eat. The other horses, less in number now than before and consisting mostly of a few retired horses, reassured him that it wasn't his memory that was at fault; the land was in a terrible drought, the likes of which had never been seen before.

This great drought was sweeping the countryside. What Keseph saw was only the beginning. Over time, the grass became drier, browner, and more brittle all over his field and many fields beyond his. For as far as the eye could see, and beyond, the drought had taken the life out of his world. The little stream, with its fresh, flowing water, stopped flowing, dried up and only left behind little puddles of muddy, stagnant water.

Stretching his neck out to reach the uneaten grass by the side of the road, Keseph spied a carriage being pulled by two, perfectly matched, silver horses. Keseph recognized their high status by the extravagant brass and by the red pompoms; he saw the majesty of each of the horses. He wondered, if the drought was as bad as the others had said, why were these horses so healthy?

The carriage horses were all strong and majestic, muscles rippling with every step they took. He saw the lovely, red pom poms shaking in the breeze; he heard the tinkling of beautiful, golden bells; he saw the golden tack of the harnesses glittering in the sun. The livery, in colours of red and gold, betokened the royal status of the carriage occupant.

After he took in the magnificence of the carriage, Keseph's gaze wandered to that of the horses. They were strong and healthy, standing with head erect. Keseph wondered again how they managed to stay strong and healthy in this drought. "Surely the drought had affected them as well," he thought. It was such a widespread drought, and more severe than any his herd had ever seen, or indeed, had even heard of in times past. But these horses, not only were they well nourished, but they were also obviously well loved and cared for. Their bearing and their confidence were a demonstration of their total well-being.

Keseph looked at his own body. Where had his muscles gone? Indeed, where had his flesh gone? He was now quite skinny, with weak, wobbly legs. His eyesight was not as good as it had been, and he now had to be careful to not run as much as he used to because his little legs felt the strain of even the smallest exercise. There was no joy in running; it hurt too much and tired him out for a long time afterward.

Keseph's attention was also drawn to a company of horses behind the royal carriage. They were no ordinary horses, either. Strong and regal looking, like the horses drawing the King's carriage, these horses were dressed for warfare. Their tack was of black leather but without the gold embellishments of the carriage horses to glint in the sunshine, thus giving away their position in battle. Neither did they have the pom poms or bells which would also be a dead give-away in battle. Their heads were protected by leather bands that came down almost to between their eyes, giving them added protection against the enemy. Their riders were all dressed in white, strange for an army, but also carrying their weapons: a sword, a shield, and a trumpet. This was a glorious army that was ready to obey their King and do exploits.

They stood as silent and as still as the carriage horses and Keseph knew (how, he wasn't quite sure) that they would respond to every command given to them, either for charging fearlessly into battle, or for standing confidently while their rider engaged in battle.

Then, like a bolt of lightning, recognition hit him: Argent was the lead horse in the team! He looked so magnificent that Keseph hardly recognized him. "Was he taller than when I left him?" thought Keseph. He looked at least three hands taller. With every muscle of his body sculpted to exact proportions, he displayed the same magnificence as the other horses in the perfectly matched team. Keseph recognised the greatness in which Argent was now walking as a carriage horse—an integral part of the King's army.

Envy came into the heart of Keseph as he compared his coltish body to Argent's magnificence. There he stood in all his glory and Keseph couldn't understand why Argent had been chosen for greatness above him. He was born for greatness, wasn't he? He was a son of a Remnant, wasn't he? As a Remnant himself, surely, he should have achieved his greatness by now. The words of the Blessing, which had so often been a comfort and an encouragement to him, were now a menace.

He wondered, "Why has my brother been so honoured, and I am neglected? Why weren't bells put on my feet when I was in training? Why didn't I have a gold embellished harness like my brother?" Regret washed over his soul. And then, when he realised the choices he made, shame replaced his regret, followed quickly be repentance. He even wondered if he really was a part of the Remnant.

Avram, knowing he was growing old and going the way of all the earth, had appointed Keseph to take his place. Keseph thought that he was a strange choice to take Avram's place. He had reverted to being a colt. Who would take notice of him in his emaciated condition? Surely there were better qualified horses to stand guard over the new foals being born. Would he even see the new foals. With the severity of the drought, no new foals had been born. The younger mares were in a separate field, sometimes fed with hay and supplied with water. Many things, he realised, were beyond his knowledge and understanding.

After Keseph had returned to his beloved fields, Avram had taken him up many times to the top of the hill under his favourite tree. His training, which had begun with the Trainer, would continue with Avram. There were still many things for

Keseph to learn and, although the method of training had changed, his training continued none the less.

Speaking as a wise father to his son, Avram had said "Keseph, you had a choice, and you made it; but what you didn't have was the ability to determine the result of your choice."

"I don't understand," Keseph had said quietly. "What about the words of the Blessing?"

"Do you remember the words?" asked Avram.

"Of course, I do. Our mother made sure we could both recite the words." His heart was pained anew as he remembered his mother, now conveyed into the second Kingdom where death and pain no longer existed. He could see himself and Argent standing with their mother beside the clearly flowing stream as she drilled them in the words of the Blessing. 'One will be destined for greatness. One will carry a harness; the other will carry freedom, but that freedom will come at a cost. One carries the excellency of dignity, majesty, and power; the other carries the beginning of strength. One bows his head to love and authority; the other has his head and his body bowed low,' he recited.

"I don't think you have remembered it well, Keseph. I believe it was 'Only one …', Avram said softly. "That makes all the difference. You assumed, in your youth and inexperience, that you were the one destined for greatness. Did you ever think about your brother?"

Keseph realised, possibly for the first time in his life, how selfish he had been. His life was so totally consumed by thoughts and actions that affected himself. He had not, once, placed the needs of anyone else above himself. He hung his head in shame. Keseph came to realize that he was an immature and untrained colt, unfit for the greatness that he thought was his by right. He also realised that, according to the words of the Blessing, his freedom had come at a cost.

"Did you not consider that the fence was there not to confine you but to keep you out of harm's way?" Avram said wisely. "It prevented you from eating the poisonous weeds that too often crept in from the outside. It prevented you from drinking water that was sometimes murky. Because you had not learned about purpose, you were not released to walk in responsibility; because you had chosen freedom over discipline, purpose, and responsibility, you must now accept the consequences." There was more that Avram could have said to Keseph, but he judged, from the look in his eyes and his low-hung head, that he had said enough.

Keseph finally realised that it was not for him to choose the consequences. No one could do that because consequences are inbuilt into every choice we make. He saw that now. He also saw how totally prideful and selfish he had become. He focussed on what he could get instead of what he could give. He focussed on his life instead of the lives of others.

Above all, he saw in retrospect the selfless love of the Trainer and His desire for relationship. It was too late to have a relationship with the Trainer but, maybe, he could develop a relationship with Avram while there was still time. Avram had been trained by the Trainer, he reasoned, so maybe the Trainer's wisdom might be passed on to him through his relationship with Avram.

As time passed, this relationship did develop. Avram imparted what he could and Keseph proved a willing and open learner. The drought ended, the grass came back fresh and green, and the streams flowed with water again. The King's field was once again lush and full of promise with the possibility of new growth. Keseph remained a colt, living in freedom, but he now carried the cost of that freedom as a mantle of wisdom. He would speak often to the new colts of the cost of freedom and the need for humility and service. There would be some who would be ready to enter the service of the King, and there would be some who would choose otherwise but, Keseph would always be available, ready to teach and exhort any who would listen, to not make the same mistake that cost him so dearly.

Author Bio

Lexia G Mackin has served God in a variety of ministries over the more than fifty years. As a trained and gifted teacher of the Word, she loves telling stories that inspire others to disciple themselves to the Word of God—Jesus being that expression.

As a result of discipling others to Jesus, with many young and not-so-young disciples, she was honoured to receive the

Family Voice Australia's 'Grandmother of the Year, 2023'.